"To see a world in a grain of sand
And a heaven in a wild flower,
Hold infinity in the palm of your hand,
And eternity in an hour."
"

~ William Blake
"Auguries Of Innocence".

Recent Publications by Angelo Letizia

Letizia, A.J.(2020) Graphic novels as pedagogy in social studies: How to draw citizenship. New York, NY; Palgrave-MacMillan Press.

Letizia, A.J. (2018) Using servant leadership: How to reframe the core functions of higher education, New Brunswick, NJ: Rutgers University Press.

Letizia, A.J. (2017) Democracy and social justice education in the information age. New York, NY: Palgrave-Macmillan Press.

Also by Angelo Letizia

The Starry Devil and Other Unwanted Poems
        Silver Bow Publishing 2021

Pilgrims
of
Infinity

by

Angelo Letizia

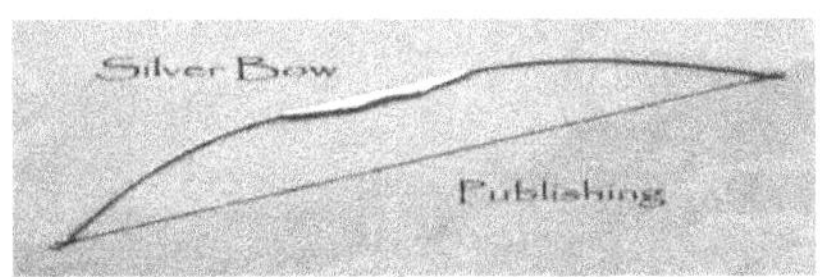

720 – Sixth Street, Box # 5
New Westminster, BC
V3C 3C5   CANADA

Title: Pilgrims of Infinity
Author: Angelo Letizia
Cover Art: "Winter's Approach" painting by Candice James
Layout and Design: Candice James
Editor: Candice James

www.silverbowpublishing.com
info@silverbowpublishing.com
© Silver Bow Publishing 2021
ISBN: 9781774031599 book
ISBN: 9781774031605 e book

Library and Archives Canada Cataloguing in Publication

Title: Pilgrims of infinity / by Angelo Letizia.
Names: Letizia, Angelo, author.
Description: Poems.
Identifiers: Canadiana (print) 20210374403 | Canadiana (ebook) 2021037442X | ISBN 9781774031599
   (softcover) | ISBN 9781774031605 (EPUB)
Classification: LCC PS3612.E79 P55 2022 | DDC 811/.6—dc23

I dedicate this book
to Jason Sullivan and Cera Steck

Contents

Foreword ... 9

History

In the Beginning ... 13
Neanderthal ... 14
Homo-Sapiens ... 15
Sumer ... 16
Egypt ... 17
Buddhism ... 18
Greece ... 19
Rome ... 20
Christianity ... 21
Dark Ages ... 22
Inquisition ... 23
Renaissance ... 24
Discovery ... 25
Enlightenment and Reason ... 26
Industry ...27
Industry II ... 28
20th Century ... 29
21st Century ... 30
The End... 31

Explorations of Infinity

Pilgrims of Infinity ... 35
Pilgrims of Infinity II ... 36
Pilgrims of Infinity III ... 37
Ceremony of Magnets ... 38
Hidden Curriculum ... 39
Aufheben... 40

Blueprint of a Black Hole ... 41
New Years ... 42
They Will Say ... 43
Graves as Signposts ... 44
Exalted ... 45
Insurrection ... 46
Unredemption... 47
Gedicht ... 48
Savior ... 49
Watching the Fields ... 50
Recollections ... 51
The Earth Reminds You ... 52
The Stone Monument ... 53
The Holy Cartographer ... 54
The Virtue of Sycophants ... 55
Certification of Bone ... 56
Author of Doubt ... 57
Desert of the Real (Baudrillard) ... 58
Advertise ... 59
Gasoline and Detergent ... 60

The Return

The Return ... 63
A Reunion of Sorts ... 64
Sherpa's Wait ... 65

Author Profile ...

Acknowledgements ...

Foreword

Are there patterns in history? Are there ideas and secrets passed down from our ancestors and through evolution? I became enthralled with these questions as I pursued my MA in European History. I found, however, it is better to utilize poetry rather than scholarship as a tool to explore these types of questions. And hence the present work before you.

The book is divided into three sections. The first section, entitled "History," surveys different historical eras in succession and proposes the premise that something, some secret, was passed down through generations. This secret, while never actually divulged (mainly because it is beyond ordinary understanding, including that of the poet) has something to do with the notion of infinity.

When we as a species (as a product of billions of years of evolution) arrive in the 21st century, that is the where the pilgrims of infinity emerge. We are finite beings that can somehow imagine the infinite, but usually do not. Perhaps it is because the finite is comfortable. Yet some brave ones however try to pierce infinity. These pilgrims, these holy explorers, are beings that can finally begin to explore this, as of yet, unintelligible secret that has developed over the course of centuries. As such, the second section of the work is appropriately titled "Explorations of Infinity." The last section charts the pilgrim's return. Make of it what you will.

There are 50 poems in this manuscript and 48 of the poems were written between the time of December 2020 and January 2021 (the poem titled: "A Reunion of Sorts" and the poem titled: "Industry II" were written in 2002 and 2003, respectively). The time of writing is important. During this time a pandemic raged out of control and the president of the United States of America tried to subvert the democratic process. How could a poet not be impacted? The poems in this book however are not merely reflections on these events- in fact these events are not directly mentioned (but readers will hear their echoes). Rather, I strove to create an all-encompassing work, which looks at history, the present and the future in totality.

What is history? It is certainly more than a static collection of facts. History is a foundation, a compass, a loadstone which points the way. History is also a repository of ideas and secrets, of philosophies and remedies, and perhaps something infinite. History is humankind's identity. Of course, there was history before humans too- we should not be so haughty. Human history is a grain of sand in the desert, 5,000 years of writing in a sea of almost 5 billion years of earth's existence.

Nevertheless, our paltry writing is perhaps a start to understanding this vastness. However, will we listen? Ironically, people today do not seem to have time for infinity or history when we need it most. Students are repeatedly told to contribute to the economy and leave esoteric and seemingly impractical pursuits like history, poetry and philosophy behind.

Will this book change any of that? Probably not. My goal was simply to begin to explore infinity and meanings in history as we trudge into an uncertain future. I do not know if I have achieved what I sought out to do, but hopefully this manuscript is a start.

Angelo J. Letizia, PhD
Manchester, MD January 2021

History

In the Beginning

There is a secret which
Stars can only whisper to cells
without words
First spoken in amoebas and nuclei
and then primates

Hominids prayed to the secret
And burnt offerings to it
The secret is a bone, a gene
A tattoo
Or skin covering

An evolution

Neanderthal

Neanderthals shiver
and bury each other.
Animal skins cover dirty flesh.

But the cave dwellers are aware.
They know the secret
of their damp and musty caves,
of their tiny universe.

And inarticulate voices
grunt the universe
in stars and fires.

Homo Sapiens

Homo Sapiens paint the secret on cave walls
and devour it in carcasses.
And then learn to
plant the secret
in fertile fields
and cultivate it with onions and wheat
so the secret can nourish civilizations
which have no name.

But these things take time.

Sumer

Babylonians study the secret,
arrange its terms and vertices,
dissect it
With an X-axis,
but they still respect it.

Cuneiform pillories the universe.
Makes it give up its innards,
arrange them in neatly chiseled rows.
Make the stars speak
in tongues we can understand
on clay tablets.

Babylonians govern the impulses
into predictable codes
and utilize teeth as collateral

Egypt

The brain is bald and vulgar.
Discard it.
Mummify the heart instead.

Thoth records
the entirety of human thought.
Weighs its merits
against
disassembled bodies and Canopic jars.

Floating universes in nitrate and knee-joints,
salt, bandages and incantations
become a currency
exchanged for the secret
and a mummified vision
preserved in an eyeball
and hieroglyph.

Buddhism

Sow celestial Buddhas in the barren soil.
This is the new agricultural revolution.
Each Buddha augments the secret
and weaves Enlightenment
between the rocks and stars.

Cultivate Mandalas in garden beds
which our progeny can reap,
in time, to feed to the markets.

Greece

Oracles are conduits
to the secret
of earth, rock and trees.

Oracles are passageways
burrowed in the universe.

Gadflies loosen tongues and release armies.
But the secret,
Opaque,
deafens all
except philosophers;
philosophers who create atoms
and heavenly archetypes ,
Starry skeletons
of secrets and thoughts.

Rome

Rotisseried door mice
revolve like planets
in a drafty solar system
of ancient villas.

The secret is slaves and patricians,
Consuls and senators
who have arranged the universe
into 12 tables
and engineered a bridge
between Mars and Neptune.

Architecture of an orderly cosmos
so the secret can bloom
when emperors die.

Christianity

A Christ walks the earth.
The baptism of forms reigns in heaven.
The holy and sacred architecture
unfolds across a depleted cartography.

But the forms are stale bread.
Celestial prison sentences that we pray to.
Manna is just dust and crumbs.
There is no more nourishment in this heaven.

Dark Ages

Peasant cottages
dot indifferent winters.
Embers are confetti
in a tapestry of soot.

But what is the purpose of these things?

Rickety stable walls
are not able to stand for long
but the horse dung underneath
Is pregnant with a secret
The illiterate peasant's harvest
cannot decipher- yet ,

Inquisition

There is something more.
Bruno saw it
amidst the echoes and economies
before the inferno of bone.

The melted bowels
of a thousand sinners shatter
as a new language is coaxed from a circle
which rings the throne.

Renaissance

Cancers and teeth.
Reborn.
Preserved in marble .
Smiling like a hungry god.

Marble fetuses gestate
grow umbilical cords of stone
to nourish these blank gods.
Vulgar gods of alone
who revel in their nascent capital slavery.

Malignant and strong
they devour the accidents
and fealty we had become.
Now profitable

Perspective dissects ancient wisdom
into embers and dust.

This time without respect,
but it clears a path

"We are born!"
the toothless starry abortion screams
and steps forward to claim the vacant thrones.

Discovery

Barnacles remember my dreams.
A dream caught in their ridges,
ridges I sailed before.

Astrolabes position me
between stars and continents .

What am I searching for?.
A symbol lapping in the frothy waves
that stink of salt in the dusty vein?
Or the water breaking
on a howling shore?

Pestilence between the teeth.
Saliva on the reef.

Trinkets cannot stall the apocalypse.

I have searched the earth for this.
The secret
and whispered back to the stars.

Enlightenment and Reason

Vinegary stars distilled into a Eucharist
administered by priests of bleach and bone
Purify the original .

Coarse skulls with no flesh
ground to glassy archetypes
who suckle at dry breasts
of a desolate church.
Of a new people and pope.

Where stringy umbilical cords
finally wither in hot dust.

"We are born again",
the efficient priest says in monotone
as he pins the secret on a board
and classifies it into genus and kingdom.

You will be happier this way,

Industry

Dirty automatons walk in patterns.
Greasy fetuses
born as cadavers with white eyes
that rise at five-thirty
to clocks they do not own.

They labor to build a plastic heaven
for someone else
with capital and paint.

Surplus value melts and replaces soil.
Titans carve holes in the forest
forget the secrets
while they reroute veins of smokestacks
to the ocean,

Industry II

Standardized parts,
interchangeable,
easily assembled and inserted
into the machine of our moon above.

Each an office or car.
A secretary
on a couch in front of a plasma TV
grinded into submission
by unceasing levers.

Humanity pours its human fuel
down the throats of her metal pets,
her beasts.
Forget the handmade parts.
They are obsolete.
Each kidney and trigger
must be made to fit any vein or gun.
But what if they assembled me wrong?

Pieces are shiny
but look exactly the same
and a gas tank was
accidentally welded to the throat.
Fuel pools behind the teeth with saliva.

I will scream and risk the spark
of grinding metal.
I can light your room better
than that dull standardized light bulb.
Even if just for a moment
in our busy lives,

20ᵗʰ Century

I am the scapegoat of centuries.
The rind of a nuclear sunset
peeled and discarded.

I am the secret tattooed in the marrow.
In the hollow cavern of bone.
In the kitchen, alone.

Turn the sausage, do not let it burn

Your stale methodologies
which are all rehearsed.

A pastiche of onions and wheat
and garbage we have seen .

The secret is a holocaust
in every home.

Where did we go wrong?

21st Century

The furniture and doors.
The glass in the mirror
became a language of sorts.
Tangible phenomes of a dusty tongue
which gives instruction
in the scientific management of
A simulacrum.

Simulacrum rearranged in neat rows
across the bowels of a television.
Vertical violent garbage flickers as carrion chimera.
Now a syntax.
An arrangement of gods in code
splayed on the linoleum
as I walk in to the kitchen

The eggs are broken
and the ovary of the refrigerator gives birth
to the simulation of a secret
But can you reprogram the wooden syllables?
Re-write and rearrange
and create a new language?
Arrange the lamps and couch
into a new grammar?
A new archetype of fabric and light?
To guide pilgrims in search of infinity?

The End?

The secret is,
there is more.
The hierarchies never hold
and turn to ash
in the furnace of the stars.

Entropy dreams
nightmares of progress
leading down a corridor
of dead galaxies and radio transmissions
where I am finally baptized
in infinity and archetypes .

This is what my ancestors carried for so long.
In their genes and graves and gave it to me.

The secret is now reborn.

A new age of poetry and meaning has dawned
silent and unrecognized
where beings of poetry and light
populate the starry insights

Pilgrims and explorers
we are once again
if we choose to be...

Explorations of Infinity

The Pilgrims of Infinity

Barren infinities add one
to the copse of rugs
in an antique shop.

There is dust here
and desolation.

There are fences and Sabbaths
which twist and break
on the iris.

There is stalled blood brimming
when the pilgrims of infinity
leech another
sarcophagus from the marrow.

Do you deny the architecture of honey?
And the drowned apples of faith?

The pilgrims of infinity
laugh at your suicides
and exorcise sins from the shroud.

All the while
your bank account overflows
with stillborn embryos.

Pilgrims of Infinity II

Where is your compact?
Your autumnal scythe?
To strike the sinners.
And the capitalists
symbols in the sea
rise like Christ .

A new watery syntax
which drowns the inches.

We can live here.
For a time.

Where the grammars of blood are drained
by the irrevocable witness.

Pilgrims of Infinity III

Mired in entrails,
an antiseptic sanctuary
gives its guillotine to the spectacle.
Glass simulacra raises its Eucharist.
Deliver us from this tragedy.

A relic of wax
which can take any form:
Descartes demon.

Plasticity is a virtue
but the headless spectacle
nurtures only the ignorant
and the bizarre
from its basket
under the scaffold.

Ceremony of Magnets

Where can I scoop the frigid air
or soil in my thumbprint?

Where can I splay the finger to see the night?
Wrap the lightning
tightly around the knuckle
to suffocate infinity.

But infinity
is an abstraction.

The brown ladder,
sawdust and gasoline,
and green paint
are infinite
celebrated in
the ceremony of magnets.

Hidden Curriculum

Curriculum wood grains
and apple ladders
arranged alphabetically
give instruction to thoughts
pregnant in the wood
now just a quarantine of relics.

(Evolution)

The curriculum of bleach
washed in each piece of steel
teaches me something new

(Evolution)

Pedagogy laced in the stars and rockets
guide the ignorant angels
who ascend
and break the hymen of heaven,

Aufheben

Starve the mortars
as they cross the blank sun.
Fashion a guillotine
out of the curriculum
to loosen the angels
and shrapnel.

But there is no redemption here
and no more buildings
in this paradise of the circle.

Only more deserts to cross.

We do not deserve
This new archeology.

Blueprint of a Black Hole

Decipher the soil
and translate the grass
so they become intelligible symbols
realigned into
some primal language.

Each utterance a portal,
an architecture of
incomprehensibility.

Each tire and computer
is a hieroglyph
and hierarchy.
A secret alphabet of windows.
A primal congregation
where logic expires.

New Years

This is an exploration .
A permutation .
An anchored constellation
in a naked universe
which motivates a stem
to touch the dome.

But there is no victory.
Just a squeal
and a folding down.

A triangle of forms.
Accordions shut.

Circles in the finger
wring a new capitalism.
Strike the toe bone.
The constellation
which sleeps
on the ground.

They Will Say

Immeasurable hallucinations
dissolve, break
on a concrete shore.

We have sacrificed the crown
to a whore
intoxicated by archeology.

East dissolves into a recollection.
Imagine the historians shudder.

Graves as Signposts

Breach the burials
and bury the syllables instead.

Parsed and incomplete vessels.
Disconnected buds which obscure the sun.

Shadows plot a revolution of noise
In the mitochondria,

Your cuneiform cannot instruct the cells.
It becomes an unintelligible curriculum.

Hieroglyphs are a dead end
of logic and dust and accountants
where we stake our tents.

Imagine instead
if language was a supplement to infinity
and not its master.

Exalted

The exodus of atoms from chaos
reconvene as worlds and syllables
where weary hominids
pin the syllables on a riverbed
and mourn their dead cousins

Celestial arches ,
crack with starlight
and span over dirty Neanderthals
as they bury their dead.

But Neanderthals
have buried the arches instead
to summon a new oracle of
logic and radio waves.

Insurrection

Naked anchors
break utopia ,
slope to the dirt.

Slouching steel demons
hold council
to pass judgement.

Reminiscent of our ancestors
and dinosaurs,
the beautiful archeology
wrenches itself free
from our museums.

And autopsies
assemble the bones
into a new starry dream,
pin the human knee with rods.

We are the new fossils.
Relics of the Anthropocene.

Unredemption

Redeem the philosophy.
Sacrifice the martyrs .
Starve the salty harbors
and sundry omens.

There are no more oracles.
Only curriculums and historians.

A weakened hymn dies
in a ring of light and a hollow sun
in this desolate century
as the vanquished reap only torment
and contradiction
sown by the ignorant.

Deliver us from reality.

Gedicht

The suicide army
resides in bleach
and glass
sowing absence in the oracle.

And prophets lament the boundary
and dissolve the atmosphere.

So we embark on a voyage
through the damaged pears.

Where are the oracles now?
Buried in garbage
as the immortal butchers carve the stars
and serve to the suicide army?

Savior

Where is your savior?
Eating pilfered meat and poisoning the bread?
Sawing the moon in half?
Rearranging grammar
into a wooden labyrinth?
Pumping sewage into the Smithsonian
and selling crucifixes?

Cheeseburger communion tablet.
Transubstantiation of fat.
Digest the flag and wait
for the next sycophant
to lead the way.

Watching the Fields

What if I was born a chimera?
Uterus of glass refracts me
as an ultraviolet wave
to take its place
in an indifferent universe
oil the stars and
grease the notion
so it slips, dripping
onto the cave wall.

There is no more room
in the universe
for Cro-Magnons,
for horns and guillotines
which are now ash
in landfills.

Recollections

Arterial geographies
networked into plaster
form a path
lead us back.

But we have been here before
to some economy
where plagues are bartered for orange rinds.
Where envy lubricates the debris
and the filaments in the firmament
crackle.

A clever subterfuge
which nonetheless
does not have
the desired effect.

The Earth Reminds You

The earth vomits up its cicadas
every 17 years
to remind us.

Peach pits and orange peels
carpet the universe
to remind us.

Rust and ash
coat the esophagus
like nicotine
to remind us.

Feces and peanut shells
are worth more
than plastic wrappers
and perhaps
are a type of currency.

But no one cares.

The Stone Monument

The idea of a sun
burns
as civilizations build pyramids
and automobiles
and stone towers
on mountains.

Celestial devils
sail between constellations
and wade between the idea of suns.
These devils trace maps
satellites do not know.

The sun will expand
and explode
and die.

But the idea of a sun
will exist
when all sentient life
is gone.

The Holy Cartographer

Propaganda slithers in the interregnum
as nascent cages gestate.
Tireless sycophants
suck a dead cartography from a cadaver.

There are only hallucinations here,
antipodes which pose as magnets and funnels,
where crusaders are wrecked
on the sacred marble.

Contagious theater nourishes the scraps,
auctions the facts
and stomachs,
sacrifices your sociology
on a makeshift altar.

The Virtue of Sycophants

Conspiracy of suicides
produces a vinegary scapegoat
and pardons the triangle.

Will you
witness the administration of gravity?
The logic of limbs?
The intricate riddle of an echo?

Lateral sanitizer scrawls its revenge
of the remote flank
in the stomach of some distant god.

Certification of Bone

Congress of bone
parsed across the spectrum.

Vanilla mystics scorn
the awkward morning
and subvert the corners
which map the marble,
engage the saboteur,
dissolve the coast into the sea,
leave the stems
to start again.

Maybe that is what we needed to see:
Birth pangs of an inverted freedom.
An insidious mitosis in January.

Author of Doubt

I can't teach the blood to flow.

Brutish logics are too effective
and terrifying.

The unruly stars
culminate into an unholy solution
to re-crucify themselves.

Sweat coats the wood
as a paradigm gestates in the column
intoxicated with propaganda and Januaries
as I prepare to ascend .

Desert of the Real (Baudrillard)

Starry alphabets echo in winter.
Manufactured scleroses
creep like frost:

A bloated rudiment
of a social contract.

A fragment
amplified across
the desert we call home.

Advertise

I cannot teach
name and thing to reconcile.

The fissure is too wide.
The breach is a swamp
which cannot mend.

There is an arrogant vigil
which breaks in the sun.
There are too many authors
and too many auctions.
The apples of infinity are muffled.

How many wax cities are advertised?
Commercial flyers wrapped around
a bald tire?

There is so much waste
and boredom
which leads to evil.

Gasoline and Detergent

Gasoline and detergent.
Carpets and checks for the landlord.

Atoms of reality
constructed and disassembled
amongst the desolate centuries.

A workshop of flesh
in every rickety shed.
Rust on the equipment
and the smell of oil.

There are secrets here
and language like architecture
and projections of cities
which materialize,
come into focus.

Bone flickers in the gutter
and delicate miracles
struggle to be born
and forgotten.

The Return

The Return

The pilgrims return.

These Sherpa's
unpack their knapsacks
and sit silently
next to the rinds and bones of infinity.

It's all they could bring back.
It's all we could understand.
It's all we deserve.

A Reunion of Sorts

The pilgrims
interact with the others
in human air.

But broken signals
sputter
between
broken pieces.

Living hearts,
exposed,
pumping bleach,
trying to cleanse
glass souls
that they know they cannot.

Sherpa's Wait

Congruent Prophets
dredge a fallow field
to retrieve a compass.

North malfeasance.

The now silent and despondent
nomads wander in the Himalayas
but still cannot find
the correct pedagogy;
and all the mandalas have rotted.

So, they accumulate compasses,
and hibernate,
waiting
for the next evolution
because this one failed.

Acknowledgements

I would like to acknowledge the close friends I have had over the course of my life and all the late night conversations over cigars. This is where true learning takes place and where this book was born.

Author Profile:

Angelo Letizia writes mainly speculative themed poetry and is currently a professor of education at a small college in Baltimore Maryland. His true passion however is poetry. *'The Starry Devil and Other Unwanted Poems'* was his debut book of poetry and 'Pilgrims of Infinity' is his second book of poetry..

Angelo's poetry has also been published in a number of literary outlets including *Tales from the Moonlit Path, Bewildering Stories, The Atlantean, Sirens Call, Red Planet, AHF Magazine, Dissections, Fevers of the Mind, Lothlorien Poetry Journal, Bindweed Magazine* and *Bowery Gothic* to name a few.

Angelo's academic credentials include:
- PhD. in Educational Policy Planning and Leadership, *College of William and Mary*
- MA. in European History, *Old Dominion University*
- BA. in Secondary Social Studies, *State University of New York* at Cortland

Angelo joined Notre Dame of Maryland in 2018 and currently teaches courses in Social Studies Methods, Curriculum, The History of American Education, The History of Higher Education, Educational Law, Leadership, and Human Development and Learning. He has also taught courses in Cultural Diversity and Strategic Planning in the past.

Angelo lives with his wife and three children in Northern Maryland.